TEN CENTS
A POUND

WRITTEN BY NHUNG N. TRAN—DAVIES
ILLUSTRATED BY JOSÉE BISAILLON

Second Story Press

Mama, I see your hands,
Coarsened and scratched,
By the twigs and bark of the trees, row on row,
By the leaves and berries, picked one by one.
I will stay with you.

Silly child, in your hands, hold these books,
Leaf through the pages and you shall see
The world beyond these mountains and our villages,
Beyond these coffee trees, row on row.
Ten cents a pound is what I'll earn
To buy these books and set you free.

But Mama, I see your feet,
Calloused and blistered,
By the dirt and gravel, step by step,
In your dusty slippers, worn through and through.
I will stay with you.

Lovely child, on your feet, wear these shoes.
They will take you upon roads that curve high and low.
Beyond these mountains and the villages,
Beyond the coffee trees, row on row.
Ten cents a pound is what I'll earn
To buy these shoes to carry you far.

Your back, Mama. I can see,
How it bends and stoops in pain
Under the weight of your work,
Day by day.
Lifting and raking, scraping and
Scouring, load by load.
I will stay with you.

Faithful child, on your shoulder is a pack,
Holding all you'll ever need to write, word by word,
About these mountains and our villages,
About the coffee trees, row on row.
Ten cents a pound is what I'll earn,
But the stories you write, though I cannot read,
Shall be worth more than gold.

What about your eyes, Mama?
Blurred and strained, through seasons wet and dry.
Sewing needles you can no longer thread, day by day.
Who will count the change, coin by coin?
I will stay with you.

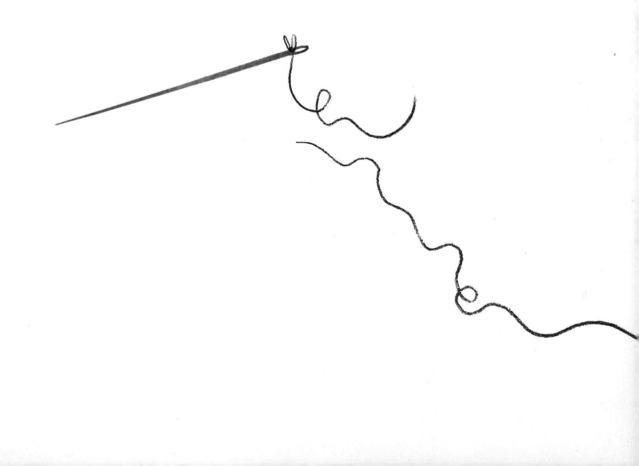

My child, listen with your ears if you refuse to see.
I am bound to these mountains and our villages,
Where the coffee grows, row on row.
For ten cents a pound is all that I know.

I hear you Mama, and now I can see.
My books and my pencils, from ten cents a pound.
To the school beyond these mountains and our villages,
I will go.

Yes, where the road winds high and low,
Is where a spirited flower like you should grow.
The sights beyond these mountains and villages
Are for you to behold.

Though it be far, where the road winds high and low,
I will come home to you, by and by.
I will come home to you, Mama,
By and by.

To our children Kenya, Monet, and Sage.
May you always see the beauty in a grain of sand.
—N. T-D.

Library and Archives Canada Cataloguing in Publication

Tran-Davies, Nhung N., author
Ten cents a pound / by Nhung N. Tran-Davies ; illustrated
by Josée Bisaillon.

ISBN 978-1-77260-056-8 (hardcover)

I. Bisaillon, Josée, 1982-, illustrator II. Title.

PS8639.R38T46 2018   jC813'.6   C2017-906247-6

Printed and bound in China

*Second Story Press gratefully acknowledges the support of the
Ontario Arts Council and the Canada Council for the Arts for our
publishing program. We acknowledge the financial support of the
Government of Canada through the Canada Book Fund.*

Published by
SECOND STORY PRESS
20 Maud Street, Suite 401
Toronto, ON M5V 2M5
www.secondstorypress.ca